THE GOAT WHO ATE EVERYTHING!

Illustration by DUCK Studios

Written by John Montgomery

Art Direction by Keith Hughes

Cover Design by Remy Glock

He was a billy goat catastrophe.
A constant eating disas-trophy.

He ate Mom's chair. He ate Dad's hair.

4

He ate the couch.
He ate the whole house.

He chomped my baseball glove with goatish delight.

He ate a streetlamp

and turned off the lights.

7

fire
hydrants

He chewed flowers and plants and

8

IRELAND

GREAT BRITAIN

GERMANY

FRANCE

We went on vacation,
and he ate all of France.

SPAIN

"Billy - you can't!"

shouted Sheriff Van Zants.

But Billy said

"BAA!"

and ate Van Zants' pants.

Suddenly, Billy let out a horrible

BELCH!!!

Billy Goat had a stomachache
like no other.

He turned
GREEN, BLUE and
EVERY COLOUR!

Billy was in an
awful mood.

Then Dad said,
"Billy, start eating
better food."

Try
LEAN PROTEIN

LOW-FAT DAIRY

 VEGETABLES

WHOLE GRAINS

 and FRUIT.

Choose the good diet, and before too long, you could grow up to be BIG and STRONG.

19

Now today, I'm proud to say,
Brother Billy is feeling great.

Although sometimes we remind him, "EAT YOUR FOOD, NOT THE PLATE!"